This book is for A

For information address Hyperion Books for Children,
114 Fifth Avenue, New York, New York 10011-5690.

First Edition
1 3 5 7 9 10 8 6 4 2
Printed in Singapore

Library of Congress Cataloging-in-Publication Data
Raschka, Christopher.
Snaily Snail / by Chris Raschka.— 1st ed.
p. cm. — (Thingy things)
Summary: Snaily snail is loved all the time, no matter what he is doing.
ISBN 0-7868-0639-7 (trade)
[1.Snails—Fiction.] I. Title.
PZ7.R1814 Sn 2000
[E]—dc21 99-51689

Visit www.hyperionchildrensbooks.com

THINGY THINGS

Snaily Snail

Chris Raschka

HYPERION BOOKS FOR CHILDREN
NEW YORK

I love you,
Snaily Snail.

I love you when
I am with you.

I love you when I am not.

I love you when
we are together.

I love you when
I am away.

I love you when
we play.

I love you when
I work.

I love you,
Snaily Snail!